Bug Sandwich

by Brady Smith

Nancy Paulsen Books

For my awesome wife, Tiffani,
who's so dang sweet the bugs
just can't leave her alone.
I love you, honey.

NANCY PAULSEN BOOKS
An imprint of Penguin Random House LLC, New York

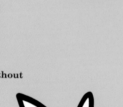

First published in the United States of America by Nancy Paulsen Books,
an imprint of Penguin Random House LLC, 2023

Copyright © 2023 by Brady Smith

Nancy Paulsen Books and colophon are trademarks of Penguin Random House LLC.
The Penguin colophon is a registered trademark of Penguin Books Limited.

Visit us online at penguinrandomhouse.com.

Library of Congress Cataloging-in-Publication Data
Names: Smith, Brady, 1971– author, illustrator.
Title: Bug sandwich / Brady Smith.
Description: New York: Nancy Paulsen Books, 2023. | Summary: "A little boy is tired of bugs biting him,
so he decides to bite back by making a bug sandwich"—Provided by publisher.
Identifiers: LCCN 2022035160 | ISBN 9780593461747 (hardcover) | ISBN 9780593461754 (ebook) | ISBN 9780593461761 (ebook)
Subjects: CYAC: Insects—Fiction. | Sandwiches—Fiction. | LCGFT: Picture Books.
Classification: LCC PZ7.1.S5955 Bu 2023 | DDC [E]—dc23
LC record available at https://lccn.loc.gov/2022035160

Manufactured in China

ISBN 9780593461747
1 3 5 7 9 10 8 6 4 2

TOPL

Edited by Nancy Paulsen
Art direction and design by Marikka Tamura
Text set in New Century Schoolbook LT Std | The art in this book was done in Procreate.

This is a story about a special kid. In fact, all kids are special, really. But what made this particular boy special is that bugs just loved him.

Nope. Unfortunately not that kind of love.

They loved to bite him!

Every day, all day, bugs bugged the boy.

He tried everything to avoid being bitten.

But nothing totally worked.

One day, the boy had an idea.

Quite possibly his best idea ever.

He was going to bite those bugs back!

He was going to make them into a BUG SANDWICH!

But first he had to catch the critters.

So he made himself a bug trapper.

I'LL GET YOU NOW, BUGGOS!

He headed out into the yard.

Hmm, funny how those critters disappear when you want them!

Hide, guys!

But those bugs didn't stay gone for long.
In fact, the backyard was full of ants.

And . . . the boy discovered
they had superstrength.

Spiders weaving webs were kind of amazing too.

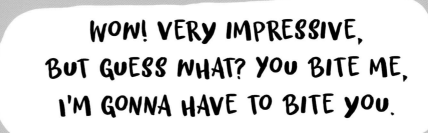

Just then, the boy heard the buzz
of a pesky mosquito.

Before he could catch it . . .

And then there were bees!
The boy couldn't believe how
they built their own house.

Soon, the boy's jar was full of bugs.
Some were quite stunning.
The boy couldn't help but be impressed.

The boy imagined that if he caught every
kind of biting bug, he'd be a national hero!
No more kids would ever have to be annoyed!

Except that while he was imagining . . .

something bit him!

Finally, it was time to make the bug sandwich.

And figure out what exactly should go on it . . .

Then it was time to BITE BACK!

The boy had never thought about it like that.
Maybe the bugs had a point?

Just then, the boy's mother called:

The bug sandwich sat on the plate—but not for long!